The Big Snow

The Big Snow

by BERTA and ELMER HADER

COLLIER BOOKS, New York, New York

Collier-Macmillan Ltd., London

The Macmillan Company, 866 Third Avenue, New York, N.Y. 10022
Collier-Macmillan Canada Ltd., Toronto, Ontario
Library of Congress catalog card number: 48–10240

The Big Snow is also published in a hardcover edition
by The Macmillan Company.
Printed in the United States of America
First Collier Books Edition 1972

1 2 3 4 5 6 7 8 9 10

F
Ha

Affectionately
dedicated to
Nancy H. G.

"Honk-honk-honk." The wild geese were flying south. The big harvest moon had come and gone. Red and gold were the leaves on the maples and oaks, and the wind that blew down from the north was cold.

Mrs. Cottontail and the littlest rabbit sat on the warm brown earth of the vegetable garden. Far below at the foot of the hill, the broad waters of the river ebbed slowly to the ocean. They stared into the sky at the flock of wild geese.

"You know what that means," said Mrs. Cottontail. The littlest rabbit shook his head. He couldn't speak because his mouth was full of carrot tops. He didn't know why the geese were flying south. This was the first time he had seen them.

"That means that the cold winter days are near and you will be needing a warm coat," said Mrs. Cottontail. "Eat plenty of cabbage leaves and carrot tops and you will have a thick coat for the winter."

The littlest rabbit nibbled another tender carrot top.

The fat little ground hog, who lived in a den just outside the garden fence, looked up as the geese flew overhead. He had already put on his warm fur coat. "Oh-oh," he said, "it's nearly time for my winter nap." When the days grew short and cold he went to bed and slept soundly until spring. This saved him the trouble of storing food for the winter.

Mrs. Chipmunk, with her cheek pouches full of seeds, stopped for a moment beside the little stone house on the hillside. She had worked hard all summer and had stored plenty of seeds and nuts for the winter in her home deep beneath the rock pile. "Brrrrr," she said, "it's getting cold. It's time for me to retire."

A blue jay perched on the topmost bough of the sycamore, looked at the geese flying in the sky high above the
river. "Well, well! It's later than I thought!" he flew to the
big pine tree where the cardinals were resting.

"Aren't you going south?" he asked.

"No, indeed," replied the cardinals, "we can find plenty to eat here. We like winter."

Song sparrows chirped happily on the hillside. They paid no attention to the geese in the sky for they did not mind the cold weather. They knew that the meadow grasses were heavy with seed and so were the birches and the ash trees.

A blue bird sat on the roof of his house built of cedar. He looked at a fat robin on the lawn below: "It's high time to go south," he called.

"Not for me," said the robin. He tugged and pulled a fine fat worm out of the ground. "I'm staying here this winter."

High on the hill a brown wood rat stopped to look at the geese. "Hey-hey," he squeaked, "there they go." He knew cold weather was coming and he had carried seeds and nuts to his nest under a big rock. The ring-necked pheasants, roaming through the woodland, only stared at him. They never thought of leaving their home for the south. There was plenty of food for them on the hill and they didn't mind the cold.

"Caw-caw-caw," croaked three black crows in the corn field, as the geese flew by. They knew where to find food during the long winter months and they never went south.

Every day during the harvest season, the red squirrels and the grey squirrels had been busy storing nuts and acorns and seeds under the leaves and logs where they hoped to find them during the lean winter months. Their fur coats were thick and warm. They were ready for winter.

The pretty white-footed wood mouse flicked his long tail as he looked at the geese flying high in the sky. He knew that winter was coming, but he had worked hard and had a good supply of seeds stored away in his underground nest. He wouldn't be hungry in the months to come.

The short-tailed meadow mouse didn't bother to look
at the geese. Winter held no terrors for him. The tunnels,
made by the moles, led to sweet plant roots and to the
tulip bulbs in the garden. He would have plenty to eat.

Shy, white-tailed deer browsed in the woods that covered the ridge at the top of the hill. Their coats were already thick and warm. Some of the deer saw the flying geese but they never thought of leaving their woodland home where there was food for all, growing so plentifully.

And there were hill-dwellers who came out to hunt for food at night. The skunk family who lived under the wood pile didn't care which way the geese were flying. They were happy and content on the hillside. There was plenty of food to be found if one only followed one's nose, and they could sleep through the coldest winter months in their bed of leaves and soft grasses.

The raccoons followed their path through the woods. They, too, knew that winter was coming. When the deep snow covered the land, they would climb into their soft bed in the hollow trunk of the old willow to sleep until the cold days passed.

The days grew shorter and shorter. Then the first snow blew down from the north. When the round winter moon bathed the hillside in silvery light, the mice and the rabbits came out to dance and frolic. The skunks, the raccoons, and the deer left well-marked trails in the early winter snow.

. . . Then the night after Christmas there was a rainbow around the moon. . . . The wise owls knew what that meant. A rainbow around the moon meant more snow. MUCH MORE. "Hoooooooooooooo," the sad trilling call of the screech owl was heard up and down and across the hillside.

The owls were right. Soft grey clouds quickly filled the sky and blotted out the moon.

A beautiful snow flake fell through the air.

Then two flakes floated softly to earth,

followed by three,

then four.

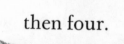

The snow flakes fell faster and faster and faster.

Millions of snow flakes fell from the sky.

It snowed all that night and all the next day. Thick snow covered the branches of all the trees.

A blanket of snow covered the meadows, the hills, the valleys.

The snow was heavy on the roofs of the houses and barns.

The snow stopped falling on the evening of the second day. Once again the big silvery moon rose high in the sky. The owls winged noiselessly from the sycamore to the pine woods. Nothing else stirred in the silent snow-covered land.

Then the skunk family dug their way up from their den buried so deep under the snow. They sniffed and sniffed but all their sharp noses smelled was snow. So they crawled back to sleep again in their soft den.

The raccoons scraped the snow away from the entrance to their home in the willow. They stared in wonder at the snow. Then they hurried back to sleep until spring in their soft warm bed.

At dawn, the jays shook their feathers and left the shelter of the big spruce. The sparrows, the chick-a-dees, the cardinals, and a lonely robin scrambled out from their shelters and flew from tree to tree, trying to find a place to perch on the heavy snow-laden branches. They looked in vain for the seed grasses in the meadow. Ice and snow covered everything, even the seeds of the birches and the ash trees.

The jays and the crows took wing to hunt for food. The jays flew north in great circles and the crows flapped slowly south.

The deer huddled together in the deep woods. Drifts of snow covered the bushes and grasses that furnished them with food. The deer were hungry.

Mrs. Cottontail and the little rabbits were hungry, too.
They came out from their nests underground to hunt for
food.

Snow, snow, nothing but snow—and the birds and the animals of the hill were very hungry.

Then the sun rose above the hills, clear and bright. The sharp eyes of the jays saw a little old man in a bright red cap come out of the stone house. He slowly shoveled a path through the deep snow.

He was followed by a little old woman dressed all in green. She scattered seeds, and nuts, and bread crumbs, to right and to left.

The cry of the blue jays echoed over the hillside. "Food, food, food," they cried, again and again. All the birds on the hill heard the happy call.

"Caw-caw-caw," croaked the crows when they saw the little old woman put pans of food back of the house, and the little old man drag hay from the shed and scatter corn on the snow.

"Food, food, food," they called and their cries were heard by the deer in the woodland away at the top of the hill. The squirrels heard them too, and raced through the tree-tops. The snow had covered their hidden stores of nuts and acorns and they were hungry. The skunk family and the raccoons, deep in their long winter sleep, did not hear the crows' call. In her warm burrow under the rock pile, the chipmunk opened a sleepy eye. She ate a few peanuts. Then she closed her eyes again to dream of the spring days to come.

All the other animals hurried as fast as they could through the snow to the little stone house.

The cardinals, the sparrows, the chick-a-dees, and the lonely robin flew to the banquet, chirping and singing. The hungry pheasants in the woods heard the glad tidings and joined the happy throng.

The ground hog didn't wake up until the second day in February. He pushed up through the snow and looked about. The sun was shining brightly and there on the snow the ground hog saw his shadow.

"Oh-oh, I know what that means," he said. "There will be six more weeks of winter." And he hurried back to his den to sleep until spring.

The ground hog was right. It was a long cold winter for the birds and animals on the hill, but the little old man and the little old woman put out food for them until the warm spring came. And that was the end of the BIG SNOW.